OLD TALES RETOLD: SPRITES AND GOBLINS

Stories of magical beings from around the world

By Marcus Pitcaithly

I0521510

To my son

John

1

First published by Marcus Pitcaithly, November 2016
© Marcus Pitcaithly 2016
ISBN (print edition): 978-0-9556864-6-7

Contents

THE GOOD NEIGHBOURS

From a Scottish legend

1:     *Myrton Castle*

Galloway used to be a land brim-full of fairies, elves, gnomes, trows, boggarts, and the like. Under every door-stone lived a helpful brownie, in every spinney a clan of mischievous bogles. Although they were mostly quite friendly, the people were a little bit afraid of them: for they loved to play practical jokes, and had a terrible temper if you upset them. Most people wouldn't even say the words "fairy" or "goblin": instead, they called them "the Good Neighbours", so as not to cause offence.

But time passed, and Scotland changed. Guns came, and black-hatted preachers who said the fairies were devils in disguise; the Stewart kings went away to England; and many of the Good Neighbours packed their bags and left. Some people started to say that they had never really existed. And if some families still left bread and milk out for the brownies that tidied their houses, others were much too busy trying to make sure they still *had* a house. Galloway had always been a wild and warlike country, whose clans – the MacCullochs, the Gordons, the Maxwells, and the rest – liked nothing better than to fight each other: but now the clan chiefs had lawyers as well as warriors, and fought with papers in the courtroom as well as with lance and musket out on the fells: so they had a new way of stealing land and cattle from each other, and from the poor common folk who had to put up with all their fighting.

Clan MacCulloch had been hurt very badly by this state of affairs. They still had two castles left, Myrton and Cardoness, but they were leaky, draughty, broken-down old places, half way to ruin. What's more, a rival chief, Sir William Gordon, had set his eyes on the two castles and what remained of the MacCulloch lands, and decided that he wanted them. His mosstroopers burned MacCulloch farms, and his clerks drew up false deeds to claim MacCulloch estates; and the MacCullochs never had a moment's peace.

Then the chief of the MacCullochs died, and Sir Godfrey MacCulloch inherited the title and the lands. When he looked into his accounts, he realised that the family had no money left: so he made a sad decision.

"I am going to sell Myrton Castle," he announced.

"Sell Myrton?" exclaimed his housekeeper, Mrs MacDowall. "What about the people who work there? Where will they live? Where will *you* live? And anyway, who'll buy it?"

"I can raise enough money to do up Myrton very nicely," said Sir Godfrey. "Once it's clean and dry and painted, the Maxwells will give me a good price for it. Then we can all move to Cardoness and do *that* up with the money I get for Myrton."

2: *The fairy knoll*

So he went down to Myrton Castle and walked all around it, with surveyors and draughtsmen and builders, working out which walls needed fixed and what should be done with the gardens: and he saw that a great green mound sat just near the castle.

"What's that?" he said. "It blocks the way to the back door and it spoils the view. What's it doing there?"

"That's a fairy knoll, Sir Godfrey," said Mrs MacDowall.

"Well, it'll have to go," said Sir Godfrey.

"Go!" blurted the housekeeper. "What do you mean, go?"

"We'll have to flatten it," said the chief surveyor. "It's in the way."

"But what about the Good Neighbours?" said the old woman, aghast.

"Good Neighbours?" scoffed the master draughtsman. "There's no such thing. Have you ever seen one?"

"Please, Sir Godfrey," said Mrs MacDowall, with tears in her eyes, "don't let them flatten the knoll."

Sir Godfrey frowned.

"Well, all right," he said, "we'll try to work round it. But if it needs to go, it needs to go."

So they carried on surveying the castle: and at the end, the chief surveyor said:

"Our main problem is the drains."

"What's wrong with the drains?" asked Sir Godfrey.

"There aren't any," said the surveyor. "All the toilets just lead down to the bottom of the castle wall. I think we should put in a drain at the back, to carry the waste away.

Look, here's a plan the master draughtsman's deputy's assistant's apprentice drew."

Sir Godfrey looked over the plan.

"But that looks as if the drain goes right through the middle of the fairy knoll," he said. "Mrs MacDowall won't like that. None of the servants will."

The chief surveyor sighed.

"We won't have to *destroy* the knoll," he said. "We'll just dig a channel through the middle of it, put the drain in, then cover it up again. It'll look just the same afterwards."

"Well," said Sir Godfrey, "I suppose that's all right."

So he gave permission to dig the drain: and the chief surveyor sent for the builders, and told them to get digging. None of the local men would do it: but there were enough workers there from other parts of Scotland, who didn't know about Myrton's fairy knoll, and didn't much care what happened there anyway, as they'd be going home when the job was done: so they started work.

3:     *The hobgoblin family*

They had no trouble putting the drain in. They found nothing buried in the mound, just earth and stones: and when the drain had been laid down, they rebuilt the knoll over it, and laid the turf down, just as it had been before. Even Mrs MacDowall had to admit that she couldn't tell it had been done.

That night, Sir Godfrey dreamt that a great tide of dirty, mucky water swept through his bedroom, washed him out of his bed, and carried him out of the window. He woke up gasping: but he was still in his own clean, warm bed. So he lay down again, and slept well for the rest of the night.

The next day, he went out riding: and, not far from Myrton, he met a hobgoblin.

The hob was less than a metre tall; he rode upon a white pony smaller than some of Sir Godfrey's hunting dogs. His ears were pointed, his clothes from cap to boots were green as the grass, and his white beard hung down as far as his knees.

"MacCulloch!" said the hobgoblin.

"That's me," said Sir Godfrey. "Who might you be?"

"I'm your neighbour," replied the hob. "My family and I have lived in the knoll behind Myrton Castle since your grandfather's grandfather's days and before, until you put that drain through it. It leaks, and it stinks! You've flooded us out of house and home!"

Sir Godfrey burst out laughing.

"But that's impossible," he said. "Nobody lives in the knoll. I was there when the workmen dug through it. There were no caves or holes or anything like that. Just earth and rocks."

"If you don't divert that drain round the outside of the knoll," said the hobgoblin, "then we'll flood you out, just as you've done to us."

Sir Godfrey remembered his dream, and he shivered.

"Show me your home," he said. "I'd like to see it."

"Get down off your horse, then," answered the hob. So Sir Godfrey got down, and tethered his horse to a tree; and the hobgoblin hopped off his pony, and, holding its reins in one hand, reached out and took Sir Godfrey's hand with the other, then stamped his foot. Suddenly the whole world seemed to be whirling around them: then Sir Godfrey landed with a loud splash in a pool of filthy water.

He looked up, blinking; then cursed as he bumped his head. He was in a house – not a cave, but a proper house, with walls of mortared stone, beds against the walls, and a hearth in the middle of the floor. It was quite like an old-fashioned Highland black house, except that there were no windows, or any daylight at all, and everything was much, much smaller. The ceiling was so low that Sir Godfrey couldn't stand up straight: that was why he had bumped his head: and the beds looked as if they were made for toddlers. There was no fire in the hearth: the ashes were sodden and turned to grey mud, and more water was pouring in from the roof. It was freezing cold, and smelt horrible.

The hob was standing next to him, the end of his beard brushing the surface of the water: and he called out:

"Come in!"

Four more hobgoblins stepped into the room: a grey-haired woman and three young ones. They were even smaller than the bearded hob, and their green clothes were splashed and stained; they were shivering, and looked utterly miserable.

"We've been happy here for over a hundred years," said the hobwife, "and now you've destroyed our home."

"I'm very sorry," said Sir Godfrey. "I had no idea."

"Didn't your housekeeper tell you?" she demanded.

"She tried to," admitted Sir Godfrey. "I should have listened. I'll have the drain diverted at once."

"You do that," she said, "and the Good Neighbours will always be your friends."

"I will," he said, "I promise."

So the bearded hob snapped his fingers, and Sir Godfrey found himself back where he had left his horse. He untethered him, jumped back into the saddle, and rode back to Myrton Castle: and he sent at once for the builders and told them to take up the drain and lay it round the outside of the knoll instead. The chief surveyor and the master draughtsman tried to argue with him; but he wouldn't take no for an answer. He made sure that the work was carried out that very day, and by evening the knoll had been put back as it was before: then he invited all the workmen into the castle for a drink to thank them for their hard work.

Down under the ground, the hobgoblins saw that the dirty water wasn't coming in any more, and knew that Sir Godfrey had kept his word: and they got to work cleaning their house.

4:     *Sir William Gordon*

The work on Myrton Castle proceeded apace, and soon it was finished: and Lord and Lady Maxwell paid Sir Godfrey a fine price for it, and he and his household moved to Cardoness. But Sir William Gordon still wanted to take the MacCulloch lands for himself: and the trouble between the two clans got worse and worse, until they were spending all their time fighting one another, and nobody had time to get the crops in or get any work done.

Then, one day, a messenger from the Gordons came to Cardoness, and said to Sir Godfrey:

"Sir William Gordon has fallen ill. He wants to make peace with you before he dies, and settle the matter of the Cardoness estates. He invites you to come to his house, and resolve your claims."

Sir Godfrey consulted Mrs MacDowall, who said:

"It would be a wonderful thing to have peace: but I don't trust the Gordons. Take your sword and pistol with you."

So Sir Godfrey armed himself, gathered up the papers that proved the MacCullochs were the lawful owners of Cardoness Castle and its lands, and rode over to Sir

William's house. Mrs MacDowall was right to be cautious: it was a trap. Sir William was not sick at all, but was lying in wait to kidnap Sir Godfrey, steal his papers, and force him to hand over all his lands. There were armed Gordons waiting in the courtyard of Sir William's house: and when Sir Godfrey rode through the gate, and saw Sir William come out of the house to meet him, he exclaimed:

"I thought you were supposed to be sick. What are you doing up and about?"

Then Sir William was nervous, because he realised Sir Godfrey had grown suspicious: and, instead of luring him into the house as he had planned, he drew his sword, and shouted to his men to attack at once. Sir Godfrey took out his pistol, and shot Sir William in the leg; then he drew his own sword, and fought his way out of the courtyard, before riding as fast as he could back to Cardoness.

The Gordons carried Sir William back into his house, laid him in his bed, and sent for doctors: but the wound was worse than it looked, and it had bled very badly. Before long, he died: and the new chieftain of the Galloway Gordons sent for the Sheriff of Wigtown, and said:

"Sir Godfrey MacCulloch was invited here for a peaceful discussion about the ownership of Cardoness, and he murdered good Sir William! He mustn't get away with this!"

So the Sheriff gave orders for Sir Godfrey to be arrested. But by the time the dragoons came to Cardoness, it was too late: as soon as Sir Godfrey had heard of Sir William Gordon's death, he had ridden down to Stranraer and taken the first boat for Ireland, for he knew what the Gordons would do. From Ireland he travelled on to France: and there he stayed.

Meanwhile, the Sheriff declared him an outlaw, never to return to Scotland. The Gordons took over Cardoness

Castle and its estates, and threw out Mrs MacDowall, and all of Sir Godfrey's old servants and his relations. All the farms attached to it were given to Gordon cousins, and the whole of Clan MacCulloch grew poor and beggarly. News of this reached Sir Godfrey in France, and he wept to hear of it.

5:     *The rescue*

Sir Godfrey stayed in France for seven years. He was safe there, because the French were enemies of the new King, and they protected outlaws and exiles from Britain; but at last he determined to return to Scotland. He wanted to see what he could do for his clansfolk, even if he couldn't get Cardoness back for himself; and he hoped that if he could gather enough evidence, he could go to the Lord Advocate in Edinburgh and get his outlawry overturned. So he booked a place on a ship, and sailed back home to Galloway.

He never did find out who betrayed him. Maybe it was the Maxwells, afraid that he would try to take back Myrton Castle as well; maybe one of the Gordon tenants recognised him, and feared that he would give their farm back to the people Sir William's heirs had driven out; or maybe one of his own clan was just too frightened to have dealings with an outlaw, or so poor that they needed the reward. Whoever it was, the Sheriff of Wigtown found him, and arrested him, and sent him in chains to Edinburgh.

There he was taken in front of the Lord Advocate, and charged with the murder of Sir William Gordon: and the Gordons made sure that plenty of witnesses were bribed to tell lies about him, and plenty who might have told the truth never got to Edinburgh. Just to make absolutely sure, they said that he had plotted against the new King as well. Their plans worked perfectly: he was found guilty, and sentenced to have his head cut off.

The next morning, he was marched out of the Tolbooth, and up the Castle Hill, where a scaffold had been built, and the executioner was waiting. Sir Godfrey made a fine long speech, explaining what had really happened, and many in the crowd wept to hear him; but at the end of it, the executioner said:

"Come along, now, sir, it's time. Kneel down."

"Now, Good Neighbours," muttered Sir Godfrey under his breath, "be my friends as you promised! One good turn deserves another."

Instantly, the little old hobgoblin appeared on his white pony, riding up the steps of the scaffold. He grabbed Sir Godfrey by the hand: and there was a rushing wind, and the world seemed to spin around until everybody felt quite dizzy: and when it was over, Sir Godfrey and the hob and the pony had disappeared.

Back at Cardoness, the Gordons were celebrating their success. By now, they were sure, their old enemy Sir Godfrey MacCulloch must be dead, and his head set over Edinburgh Castle gate: so they were feasting and drinking and laughing, sure that the MacCullochs would never challenge their claim to the lands again.

Suddenly, Sir Godfrey appeared in their very midst. He snatched his old claymore off the wall, and shouted:

"Be off with you all, back to your own lands, or you'll be the ones whose heads get chopped off!"

The Gordons screamed in terror, certain that this must be Sir Godfrey's angry ghost, come back to avenge his death. They ran back and forth, flapping about like chickens: and every time one of them tried to go for a weapon, the hobwife would leap out in front of him, or one

13

of the little hoblings would trip him up, until they were certain that all the hosts of Fairyland had come to help Sir Godfrey's ghost. At last every one of them fled from the castle, shrieking that it was haunted: and they never dared go back there. The castle was left empty and abandoned, and today it's a ruin.

After that, nobody saw Sir Godfrey MacCulloch ever again; most likely he went to live with the Good Neighbours. For all I know, he's still living with them.

TATTERHOOD AND THE TROLLS

From a Norwegian folk tale

1:   *The Queen wants a child*

Long ago, there lived a King and Queen in Norway who had no children. This made them very sad: their castle was a dull and lifeless place, and there would be nobody to take over the kingdom when they died.

Wherever they travelled in their kingdom, they saw children. Happy, laughing children running and playing; but also poor and hungry children, whom the Queen dearly wanted to help. In every town they passed through, she would give a feast for the poor children; and she wept to see them, so thin and ragged. The Lord Chamberlain used to fuss and tut, and say:

"This is costing a lot of money, Your Majesties. What good does the kingdom get out of feeding those children? What use are they?"

But the King just hummed and hawed, and said:

"It pleases the Queen." And the Queen said:

"It is the right thing to do. Would you let them starve to death?"

At last she went to the King, and said:

"I can't bear the emptiness of this castle any more. If we can't have a child of our own, we should adopt one. My cousin Gytha died not long ago; her little daughter Hilda has no parents. Why don't we take her in, and bring her up as a princess?"

So the King agreed; and little Hilda came to live in the castle. The Queen doted on her, and spoiled her, and gave her everything she asked for: soon the castle was filled with toys, and the Lord Chamberlain kept tripping over them, and became grumpier than ever.

But because the Queen gave all her attention to Hilda, she forgot about the poor children she used to help. Now, when she saw a ragged child, she would say:

"Tsk, tsk! What a dirty little thing! Not like our beautiful Hilda."

One day, she looked down from the castle window, and saw little Hilda in the courtyard, playing catch with another little girl she had never seen before. The other girl was obviously a poor peasant, and her clothes were dirty and ragged; and the Queen thought to herself:

"This won't do at all!"

So she lent out of the window, and called out:

"Hilda! Come up here at once!"

So Hilda ran into the castle; but she took her new friend with her, and they went up to the Queen's room together. When they came in, the Queen said:

"Little girl, you shouldn't be here without permission. Where are your mother and father?"

"My mother is selling eggs in the town," said the girl. "I don't have a father."

"Well, go and help your mother sell eggs, then," said the Queen. "Hilda, I don't want you hanging around little ragamuffins like this. Imagine what the Lord Chamberlain would say! There are plenty of nice children who would love to be friends with a princess."

Hilda was nearly crying at the thought of being parted from her friend: but the little ragged girl wasn't afraid of the Queen. She stepped forward, and said boldly:

"You wouldn't send me away if you knew what my mother could do for you."

"Whatever do you mean?" exclaimed the Queen.

"Send for my mother, and give her a cup of wine," said the little girl; "and she'll make it so you can have children of your own."

2:     *The two flowers*

At once the Queen sent servants down into the town to find the egg seller. They soon found her, going from door to door with her basket of eggs, and they brought her back up to the castle: and the Queen said to her:

"Your daughter says you can make it possible for me to have children. Is that true?"

"It's all lies," said the egg seller. "She shouldn't go saying such things."

17

In fact, it was true. The egg seller was a witch, and quite a powerful one in a small way. But although she was a good witch, she knew that most people thought all witches were bad, so she was afraid that she would get in trouble if the Queen knew about her magic. But the Queen was cunning: and she remembered that the little girl had said to give her mother a cup of wine first. So she sent for some, and said to the egg seller:

"Here, have a drink with me."

The egg seller was very honoured to be drinking with the Queen, and she was very fond of good wine: so she guzzled it down. Then the Queen said:

"Now, tell me again: is it true that you can make it so I can have children?"

"There is a way," said the egg seller. "Have two pails of water brought up to your room before you go to bed; wash your face first in one, and then the other, then pour the water out onto the floor. When you wake up in the morning, there'll be two flowers growing there, a fine pink one and a rotten-looking black one. Eat the pink flower, and within a year you'll have a baby girl: but throw the black flower away, for there'll be dangerous magic in that one."

The Queen was overjoyed; she heaped the egg seller with gold, and said her daughter could come to the castle and play with Princess Hilda whenever she liked. That very night, she did as the egg seller had said: she washed her face from the two pails of water, then poured the rest out on the bedroom floor. The King grumbled and said he didn't see any point in making such a mess, but she ignored him: and when they woke up in the morning, there were the two flowers, just as the witch had said.

The pink flower was tall and straight and fragrant, and it almost seemed a shame to eat it; but the Queen was so excited that she snatched it up and gobbled it down almost without thinking.

It was the sweetest thing she had ever tasted: but it was so light and thin, and gone so soon, that it left the Queen desperate for more. She looked at the black flower, which was twisted and slimy and smelt sour: and she thought to herself:

"It can't be as bad as it looks. It grew from the same water as the pink flower: I'm sure it tastes a little bit like it. What harm can it do?"

And so she picked the black flower, and ate that too. It actually didn't taste bad at all, though it was nothing like the pink flower, but rich and savoury where the pink one had been sweet.

Just as the witch had promised, the Queen became pregnant: and eventually her baby was born. But a strange looking baby she was! She had a snub nose, and a sallow face, and a tangle of red hair: and at the moment she was born a great nanny goat came clattering into the room. Nobody knew where it had come from: but the baby got up, and jumped on its back, and shouted:

"Mama!"

Then the doctor and the midwife started muttering, because who ever heard of a newborn baby that could talk, and jump, and ride a goat? And the Queen exclaimed:

"What evil magic is this? Is this little monster my daughter?"

"Oh, don't worry," said the baby. "My sister will be along soon, and you'll like her much better."

"She's right," said the midwife. "You're having twins."

So the second baby was delivered: and this one was a pretty little thing with golden hair, who didn't jump around or talk, but lay in her mother's arms like an ordinary baby.

They called the golden-haired girl Astrid; but they didn't give her elder sister a name, because the midwife said:

"A girl who can walk and talk as soon as she's born must find a name for herself."

3:    *The trolls' party*

The years went by, and the two sisters grew up. Astrid was always a proper little princess, and dressed neatly, and did as her parents told her: but the older twin was just the opposite. She was a messy, mucky, careless creature, who did as she pleased. She used to ride about everywhere on her nanny goat, Wilhelmina, who grew as she did, and was as big as a pony by the time she was in her teens; and she always carried her wooden spoon in her hands. Whenever the Queen and servants tried to comb her hair, it would be wild and dirty again an hour later; whenever they put her in bright, pretty dresses, she would soon get them torn to shreds climbing trees. She usually wore tatty old clothes instead; so people nicknamed her "Tatterhood". Because she still didn't have a real name, she said:

"That's as good a name as any. I'll be Tatterhood from now on."

But although the twins were so different, they loved each other dearly, and nobody could ever keep them apart. Hilda was grown up by now, and spent her time travelling around Norway, taking care of the poor children as the Queen used to do; so she wasn't around when the trolls came to court.

It was many years since the King and Queen had met with trolls. The princesses had never really seen one, though Tatterhood thought she might have glimpsed a few in the shadows when she went riding on Wilhelmina in the forest. In fact, most young people they knew weren't at all sure that trolls existed. It was a long time since they had come out on Christmas Eve to party in a human house, and longer still since they had dared come to the castle.

But now, they came. Huge stony Mountain Trolls with moss and small shrubs growing on their bodies broke open the gates; three-eyed Trows in their grey coats came out from the ancient burial mounds; tiny mischievous Nisse streamed up from the fields; great hairy Forest Trolls and their weirdly beautiful Huldra daughters came out of the woods, their long tails swishing behind them; wicked little Underground Trolls crept out of their holes; even the scaly Sea Troll and her children came, all covered in weeds and slime, to join the party.

The trolls took over the great hall of the castle, while all the courtiers and servants and guards ran and hid; and they smashed the King's best plates and crushed the Queen's finest glasses, and drank wine and ale straight from the barrels, and pulled all the food they could find out of the larder and ate it up, throwing bones on the floor, and laughing and shrieking.

When the food was gone, one of the Mountain Trolls growled:

"I'm still hungry. I wish those people hadn't run away; they looked tasty."

"I'm sure they're still hiding somewhere," said an Underground Troll, with an evil grin.

"The King has plenty of cattle and goats," said a Nisse hurriedly. Trows and Nisse are friendly to people, and she didn't want to let the Mountain Troll eat anyone. "We'll bring some of them in for you."

So the Nisse went and rounded up the animals. Meanwhile, upstairs, the Queen had hidden her daughters in her room, and told them to be as quiet as could be: and they could hear all the raucous noise of the trolls' party. Astrid was terrified; but Tatterhood was just angry that they were ruining Christmas and smashing up her parents' things. At last, she exclaimed:

"I'm going out there! If none of Father's soldiers is brave enough to drive the trolls away, I'll just have to do it myself!"

"No!" said the Queen. "Please, stay here! It's much too dangerous!"

"Listen to Mother!" added Astrid. "They'll tear you to pieces!"

"It'll take more than trolls to kill me," said Tatterhood. "Wasn't I born from the magic black flower? Didn't I walk and talk as soon as I was born? I'll round those trolls up and drive them out like a flock of sheep. But you two stay in here, and mind you keep the door shut until I tell you it's safe."

There was nothing they could do to stop her: so she picked up her wooden spoon, climbed onto Wilhelmina – who was hiding in the bedroom with them – and rode out, and down the stairs into the great hall.

The Nisse were just driving the cows into the hall when Tatterhood appeared. When the hungry Mountain Troll saw her, he licked his lips, and said:

"Oh good – you've brought me a big goat *and* a nice tasty girl!"

But Tatterhood rode up to him, and bashed him on the head with her wooden spoon: and he felt as if a tree had fallen on his head. He howled with pain: and Tatterhood urged the goat to a gallop, and rode round and round the hall, hitting every troll within reach. Soon dozens of them were dazed and groaning: and she shouted:

"Out! Get out! All of you! This is my house, and you weren't invited!"

The trolls were amazed that a human would stand up to them, and could hardly believe that an ordinary wooden spoon hurt so much: but they were all afraid of Tatterhood hitting them again, so they got up, one by one, and started to tramp towards the door.

Back in the Queen's bedroom, Astrid sighed, and said:

"Tatterhood is so brave! It must be a fine sight, her driving off a whole pack of trolls like that. I wish I could see it!"

"Well, we can't," said her mother. "We have to stay in here until they've all gone."

"Just a peek," said Astrid. "They won't notice me – they're too busy with Tatterhood." And she opened the door, just a crack, and poked her head round it.

It chanced that the wicked little Underground Troll was looking up at the landing just then: and when she saw Astrid, she snatched the head off one of the cows the Nisse had brought in, and jumped such a jump that she landed right on the landing: and she grabbed Astrid by the hair, and said:

"By spindle, flax, and thread, I'll have your head!"

And suddenly, it was Astrid's head in her hand, and poor Astrid had a cow's head on her shoulders. The Underground Troll cackled with glee, stuffed the head in a sack, and jumped out of a window; and all Astrid could say was "moo!"

23

When Tatterhood came back upstairs, and found her sister with a cow's head, sitting on the ground and mooing, she knew at once what must have happened: and she scolded her mother for not taking better care of Astrid. The Queen could only weep and wring her hands; and the King said:

"You should have stayed in the bedroom, Tatterhood. The trolls would have gone away on Christmas morning."

"So you think it's my fault, do you?" snapped Tatterhood. "Very well, then: I'll put it right."

"How will you do that?" demanded the King.

"There's only one place where they know how to undo troll magic," said Tatterhood. "That's Geirrod's Gard, the troll city, in the Utmost North. Give me a ship, with good store of food, drink, and weapons, and I'll take her there and find a cure."

"I can't let you go to such a dangerous place," said the King, "much less take your sister, especially in her condition."

"I'm the only person who's ever got the better of the trolls," said Tatterhood. "And if I don't take Astrid with me, how am I going to cure her?"

"All right," said the King, who could see that his daughter was a brave and resourceful girl, and a match for any troll. "Which of my captains would you like to command your ship?"

"I don't need a captain," said Tatterhood. "I don't even need a crew. I'll sail it myself. I won't take anybody with me but Astrid and Wilhelmina."

So the King gave in, and ordered a ship to be prepared: and when it was ready, Tatterhood took Astrid and the goat aboard, and cast off. She sailed round the southern tip of Norway, then up the coast, past hundreds of fjords, and into the frozen lands of the north: until at last they came to Geirrod's Gard, the city of the trolls. The city lay deep in a gloomy valley, where the sun's rays never reached it: the buildings were made from great unshaped boulders piled together, and lit by fire burning in huge braziers. There was a landing stage at the foot of the valley, where the icy river met the sea: and there Tatterhood tied up her ship.

"Stay below decks," she told her sister. "I'm going into town to see what I can find out."

"Moo," agreed Astrid.

So Tatterhood mounted on Wilhelmina's back, and rode up the valley to Geirrod's Gard, making for the palace of the Mountain King, which was carved into the living rock at the head of the valley. There, on a window ledge, she saw her sister's head, displayed so that all the trolls could see what the wicked Underground Troll had done: and when the head saw Tatterhood, it whispered:

"Save me!"

"Come on, Wilhelmina," said Tatterhood. "Jump!"

So up the goat jumped, higher than she had ever jumped before; and at the top of her leap, Tatterhood reached through the window, and snatched Astrid's head from the ledge.

Before she had even landed, the trolls knew the head was gone: and out of the palace and their low stone houses they came in a rush, like a nestful of angry ants. Wilhelmina kicked and butted and bit, and Tatterhood laid about them with her wooden spoon: and at last they managed to fight their way down to the bottom of the valley, and into the sunlight. All trolls fear the sun: so they gave up, and went home, and Wilhelmina carried Tatterhood and Astrid's head safely onto the ship.

Tatterhood went into the cabin where her sister was waiting.

"Moo!" Astrid greeted her. "Moo moo?"

"Yes, I've got it!" said Tatterhood. She held up the head, and put her other hand on Astrid's cow-head: and she said: "By spindle, flax, and thread, here's your head!" And with that, Astrid's head was magicked back onto her own neck again.

5:    *The Prince of Permia*

Astrid hugged her sister, and said:

"Thank you, thank you, thank you! Now can we go home?"

"In a bit," said Tatterhood. "Don't you want to see more of the Utmost North while we're here? How would you like to visit the King of the Permians?" Astrid agreed that this sounded exciting: so they set sail for Permia.

When the King of the Permians heard that a strange ship had arrived, crewed only by two women, and one of them rode a giant goat and carried a wooden spoon, he was very puzzled. But because he was a polite man, he sent messengers down to ask the sisters who they were, and if they would like to come up to his longhouse for dinner.

"Only if the King himself comes to ask us," said Tatterhood; so the messengers went back to the King. He was so curious that he did go down to the ship, and ask the sisters in person to come to dinner.

They accepted; and over dinner, they told the King and his family all about their adventures. The more they talked, the more the Astrid and the King gazed into one another's eyes; and at the end of the evening, the King said:

"There is nothing that would make me happier than if Princess Astrid would stay in Permia and be my wife."

"I would love to," said the Princess. "But I can't leave my sister to go back to Norway on her own. Besides, the custom in Norway is that the eldest should be married first."

"Very well," said the King. "Tatterhood, will you marry my brother, Prince Asko?"

Tatterhood and the Prince both readily agreed: and preparations were made for the double wedding. But when the day came, and Astrid rode out on a horse from the King's stables, wearing a beautiful white gown, Tatterhood turned up looking as messy and ragged as ever, and still riding on the back of her goat and brandishing her wooden spoon. Prince Asko tried not to look disappointed: he had been so looking forward to seeing her in pretty clothes like her sister's: but he said nothing. In fact, he didn't speak all the way to the church: until at last Tatterhood asked him:

"Why are you so silent? Today is a happy day."

"Why do you ride that old goat instead of a horse?" exclaimed the Prince.

"What goat is that?" asked Tatterhood. "Wilhelmina is the finest white mare you ever saw." And he looked, and saw that the goat had turned into a beautiful mare.

The Prince was startled: but he said:

"Well then, why do you carry that ridiculous wooden spoon?"

"What wooden spoon?" said Tatterhood. "I'm carrying a silver sceptre, bright as a fairy wand." And so she was.

They rode on for a bit longer; then Tatterhood said:

"Aren't you going to ask why I go about looking such a mess, in ragged clothes and with dirty hair?"

"No," said the Prince. "Obviously you choose to, and you'll change them when you want to."

"Look at me again," said Tatterhood. And Prince Asko looked at her: and her whole appearance had changed. Her ragged kirtle was now a gown of green velvet, edged with pearls; her greyish skin had turned fine and clear; the dirt and the tangles were gone from her hair; and if her curls were still wild and her nose still turned up at the end, Prince Asko wouldn't have it any other way, for in his eyes she was far prettier than her sister. And the tattered old hood that had given her her name was turned into a crown of shining gold: and it was a beautiful sight they made when they went into the church.

After the wedding feast, the two couples went to Norway to visit the girls' parents: and very glad they were to see them safe and happy, and Astrid with her own head back on again. But when Astrid and her husband went back to Permia, Asko and Tatterhood went travelling together, and had adventures all over the world. They didn't want to ever be a king and queen: so Tatterhood's parents declared that Hilda would be Queen when they died. She was a good Queen, and had a long and happy reign: but that's another story.

THE SKY PEOPLE

From a Tlingit folk tale

1:     *Two friends*

Long ago, in what's now southern Alaska, there lived
two boys of the Tlingit nation.

Gush was the son of a clan chief; Katishan lived on the other side of their village. They were best friends, and loved to play together, pretending that they were hunting moose or bears, or that they could fly to the moon. They would make hundreds of blunt toy arrows, and have shooting competitions, trying to see who could be the first to hit the highest branch of a tree, or a pebble on top of a wall.

One evening, they had met on a hilltop outside the village to shoot by moonlight. They had both lugged great bundles of arrows along with them; they had used up every straight stick they could find, just to see who could make more.

The moon was full that night, and bathed the whole hill in pale light.

"Isn't it beautiful," said Gush. "Wouldn't it be wonderful to fly up there and visit the Moon Chief?"

"You're always talking about going to the moon," said Katishan. "It doesn't look anything special to me; the bar my mother wears through her lip is bigger and shinier than that."

"Don't talk like that!" said Gush. "The Moon Chief will hear you."

"I don't believe there is a Moon Chief," said Katishan scornfully.

Then, suddenly, the face of the moon went black; and a ring of light circled round the two young friends, in all the colours of the rainbow, and lifted them off the ground.

Just as suddenly, it vanished, and Gush fell back down on the hillside. The moon was shining again; but Katishan was nowhere to be seen.

"Katishan!" called Gush. "Katishan! Where are you? Don't play tricks; come on out." But there was no answer.

Gush ran back up to the hilltop. The moon lit up all the land around, but he couldn't see any sign of his friend. Then Gush had a terrible thought.

"The Moon Chief must have carried him off," he said to himself. "I warned him not to make him angry! Now I'll never see him again." And he sat down and cried.

2: *Gush climbs to the Sky Country*

Gush cried until he had no tears left: but by now his sadness had turned to anger. He stood up, picked up his bow, and loosed an arrow straight at the moon.

He watched the arrow fly up into the sky: but instead of coming down, it kept on going, until at last it disappeared. Gush rubbed his eyes. He took another arrow, and aimed at the bright little star next to the moon: and when he loosed his arrow, it flew straight up, and put the star out.

"My arrows are going all the way up to the Sky Country!" Gush realised. He took aim at the moon again, and fired arrow after arrow after arrow. Each arrow he loosed hit the end of the one before: and at last the chain of arrows grew so long that he could see the end of it in the sky above him. He loosed the last few arrows, and they stuck in the end of the chain like the rest.

Gush looked about him. He hadn't eaten all night, and it was nearly dawn: and he knew he would have to take some food with him. Nearby, he saw a huckleberry bush: but the berries weren't ripe yet, because it was the wrong time of year. But since there was nothing else to eat, he pulled the bush up by the roots, and put it on his back. Then, with a great leap, he jumped up, caught hold of the last arrow, and pulled himself up onto the chain: and he started to climb.

He climbed and climbed, for what felt like days. When he got too hungry to climb any more without food, he got the huckleberry bush off his back: and he was surprised to see that the berries were rich and ripe. Because he'd been climbing up into the sky, he was closer to the sun: so the summer came earlier and the berries ripened faster. He ate all he could, then set off again.

When he felt hungry again, he got the bush down, and found that a whole new crop of huckleberries had grown and ripened while he'd been climbing. So he ate them all, and went on. At last, after he'd eaten the third crop of berries, and was too exhausted to climb any further, he came to the Sky Country. He found himself by the side of a lake: and he lay down there, covered himself with bracken and moss to keep warm, and went to sleep.

3:     *Gush meets the Sky People*

Gush slept far longer than he meant to: and he woke up to find a girl leaning over him and shaking him. She looked quite unlike anybody he'd ever seen before: she was very small, with pointed features and bright yellow eyes, and her skin seemed to give off a soft glow. She was dressed in brightly coloured skins, decorated with quills like a porcupine's.

With a shock, Gush realised that she was not human, but must be one of the Sky People. He scrambled backwards in fear, and exclaimed:

"What do you want?"

"I want you to come with me to my granny's house, of course," she said, as if it was obvious.

"Why?" said Gush.

"Because you're in danger here, sleeping out in the open. Imagine if the Moon Chief found you!"

"The Moon Chief has captured my friend," said Gush. "That's why I'm here."

"Then that's all the more reason why you should come with me," said the Sky Girl. "You can't rescue him on your own, but Grandmother can help you. She is the medicine woman of the Sky People."

So Gush followed the girl over the strange, alien landscape of the Sky Country, to her grandmother's hut: and she knocked on the door, and the old woman let them both in. He had to bend very low to get in the door, and couldn't stand up properly inside, because the Sky People were so little: so he sat on the ground, and thanked the medicine woman for her hospitality.

"You have come a long way," she said. "It is many hundreds of years since anyone climbed up from Earth to our country. What have you come looking for?"

"My friend Katishan was carried off by the Moon Chief," he said. "I have come to find him."

"Ah!" said the old woman. "I know the boy you mean. He is held prisoner in the Moon Chief's house, not a stone's throw from here. At night I can hear him crying."

"Then we must rescue him right away!" exclaimed Gush.

"You can rescue him tonight, when it is dark," said the old Sky Woman. "First you must eat; you look starving." Gush looked around: he could see no food in the bare little hut, and he did not know what the Sky People ate. But the old grandmother smiled, and said: "I can conjure up a good meal for a growing human boy, never you worry." She put her hand in front of her mouth, and whispered some magic words which Gush couldn't hear: and at once a poached salmon appeared, garnished with salmonberries and foamberries. Gush ate and ate until he was full, while the kindly old Sky Woman looked smilingly on.

4:      *The rescue of Katishan*

When the sun had set, the old medicine woman said to Gush:

"Soon the Moon Chief and his guards will be in bed, and you can go to rescue your friend. But you must take some things with you." And she handed him a spruce cone; a little rose bush in a pot; a stick of devil's-club, which is a spiny shrub that flowers in Alaska; and a whetstone.

"Well, thank you," said Gush, "but how will these be any use? Surely I need weapons and ropes and armour more than spruce cones and flowers?"

"The Moon Chief's house is small enough for a big human boy like you to climb up the roof without a rope," she said, "and you can pull your friend out through the chimney-hole. It's afterwards that you'll need these four things. If the Moon Chief's warriors chase you, throw one of these behind you, and you'll soon see how much use they are."

So she pointed him the way to the Moon Chief's house, and he crept up towards it, taking care not to be seen. When he got there, he found that the Sky Woman had been right: the roof was so low that he could easily clamber up onto it, and pull himself up towards the smoke-hole. When he got there, and peered down into the hazy darkness, he saw Katishan right below the smoke-hole: the cruel Moon Chief had tied him up and slung him from the rafters above his fire. Down below, the Moon Chief and his servants were sleeping. The Moon Chief was the tallest of all the Sky People, and had a huge belly and a white face: in fact, he was as round and pale as the moon itself.

Gush reached down, and pulled his friend out through the chimney-hole.

"However did you get to the moon?" wondered Katishan.

"Hush," said Gush. "We have to get home before the Moon Chief's people catch us." And he untied Katishan, tied the spruce cone on the end of the rope in his place, and dropped it back into the Moon Chief's house.

While the two boys climbed down the roof and started to make for the place where the arrow-ladder began, the spruce cone cried and whimpered, imitating Katishan's voice, so that the Moon People should not realise he had gone. For a while, this worked: but after a few minutes, the Moon Chief went to tell the captive boy to be quiet so he could sleep, and he found just the spruce cone there.

"Get up!" he shouted, stamping his foot. "The human has escaped! We must find him!"

So the Moon Chief's guards came running, and set off to follow the trail of Gush and Katishan: and soon they saw them, running across the plains of the moon.

"There they are!" barked the Moon Chief. "Catch them!"

Then Gush remembered what the old Sky Woman had told him: and he took the stick of devil's-club and threw it back towards the pursuing Moon People. Where it hit the ground, a great thorny patch of devil's-club sprang up, barring the way: the Moon Chief and his followers had to draw their knives and hack their way through, while the spines scratched them and caught at their clothes; and all the while the two Tlingit boys got further away, so that when the Moon People finally won through the shrubs they were just specks in the distance.

"Faster!" yelled the Moon Chief, jumping up and down on the spot in fury. "We're faster than humans – we can still get them!"

So the Moon People raced on: and they steadily gained on the two boys. By this time, Katishan, who was tired and hungry and sore, was flagging; and he said:

"I can't go any faster; they'll catch us for sure."

But Gush threw the rose bush behind them, and a great thorny hedge sprang up, twice as thick as the devil's-club and three times as spiky, and blocked the Moon People's way. The Moon Chief shouted and cursed, and ordered his men to cut it down: but while they were fighting their way through the rose hedge, the two boys reached the chain of arrows, and began to climb along it towards the Earth.

5:     *Escape to Earth*

The Moon Chief and his men had at last cut their way through the rose hedge, and they saw the boys climbing into the sky along the chain of arrows.

"It's too late," said one of the warriors. "They've got away."

"Climb after them!" screamed the Moon Chief. "We're far more agile than these great clumsy humans!"

But when Gush saw them come to the bottom of the arrow-ladder, he took out the whetstone the old Sky Woman had given him, and threw it down at them. When it hit the ground, it turned into a huge cliff, so that the Moon People couldn't reach the arrow-ladder: but the ladder itself came adrift, and was so badly shaken that the two boys fell off, and landed back by the lake where Gush had first arrived; and they sat down and cried, for although they were safe from the Moon Chief now, their ladder of arrows was drifting off into space.

"What are you crying about?" said a voice. They looked up, and saw the Sky Girl, with her grandmother standing behind her.

"We can't get home!" exclaimed Gush. "We're trapped here for ever!"

"You'll get home soon enough," said the old medicine woman. "But first you need food and rest. You could never have climbed all the way back to Earth in the state you're in, anyway."

So she took them home, and gave them a meal, and they slept for a few hours; then she said:

"Now, go back to the lakeside, lie down, and close your eyes: and think of the hilltop where you were playing with your bows and arrows before you came here."

So they did as she had said: but their thoughts were mixed up, because they couldn't help thinking of all their adventures in the Sky Country, and how kind the old medicine woman had been: and when they opened their eyes they found themselves back in her house.

"You didn't keep your minds on the hilltop, did you?" she said. "Go and lie down again, and this time think of nothing else."

So once again they did as she said: and this time, when they opened their eyes, they found themselves back on the hilltop where they had played their shooting game. They leapt joyfully to their feet, and rushed back to the village: and the first person they met was Gush's little brother.

"Gush! Katishan!" he exclaimed. "You're alive!"

"Of course we're alive," said Gush.

"The whole village is in mourning! You've been missing for over a week – we all thought you had been eaten by bears!"

So the little boy led his brother and his friend back into the village; and their families came out, and hugged them, and cried; and everybody rejoiced to have them back, and marvelled to hear the story of their adventures.

After that time, the Moon Chief seemed to lose most of his powers. Perhaps it's because he's trapped behind the cliff; or perhaps the wise old medicine woman, whose magic was stronger than his, took them away from him; or perhaps it's just because he learned his lesson. But whatever the reason is, he has never hurt another human being since that time.

In fact, he became so scared of humans that, when the first astronauts flew to the moon, he ordered all his people to hide: and they didn't see a single Sky Person the whole time they were there.

THE RIVER DEMONS

From a Ukrainian-Jewish folk tale

1:     *How the quarrel began*

In a little village, on the banks of the Horyń River in the Radyvyliv District of old Ukraine, there lived a miller named Azriel Brisker. He rented his mill from the government, and life wasn't easy: but he was a canny and hard-working man, and his wife and son helped him out:

and they lived well enough. Every farmer in those parts brought their grain to Azriel's mill to be ground, and they supplied flour to the whole village; and often they had more than they could sell there.

When that happened, Azriel and his son Sholem would take the extra flour into Radyvyliv town to sell in the market. They always stayed at the same inn, which belonged to a man from their village named Yakov Reiff, and his wife Feige. Yakov used to welcome them warmly; he gave them a discount on their rooms, and bought plenty of flour from them, and he even asked them to dine with his family. That's how Sholem met Golde.

Golde Reiff was Yakov's eldest daughter. She was lovely and charming, and she liked all the same things Sholem did, from the same food to the same books: and it wasn't long before the two young people fell in love.

When Golde told her parents that she wanted to marry Sholem Brisker, her mother said:

"But the Briskers are just country folk. You could find a rich merchant in Rivne, or a scholar in Kiev."

But her father said:

"The Briskers are good people. Besides, I would like it if she married somebody from my old village. I'll go and speak to Azriel and make the arrangements."

Meanwhile, back in the village, Sholem had spoken to his parents as well. His mother was delighted; but his father shook his head, and said:

"I can't allow it."

"What!" exclaimed Sholem. "Why ever not?"

"Because I don't approve of Yakov Reiff, and what's more I don't trust him," said the miller. "He didn't get rich honestly. He waters down his beer and never pays the brewers; he bullies his staff; he overcharges; and nobody can do anything about it, because he bribes the magistrate."

"All this may be true," said Sholem, "but I want to marry Golde, not her father."

"I'm sorry," said Azriel. "You can't, and that's final."

So, when Yakov Reiff rode out from Radyvyliv to Azriel's mill, thinking that he'd soon be celebrating the good news with the Briskers, the miller told him to go away. The innkeeper was speechless; nobody had ever turned him away before. He rode away in a fury, vowing to get revenge on the Brisker family.

2:     *Yakov takes the mill*

Yakov stormed back into the inn, red in the face and stamping his feet. When Feige saw him, she asked what had happened: and he shouted:

"Who does that miller think he is? He'd be lucky if his son did get to marry into our family! How dare he turn us down? I'll get my own back, mark my words!"

When Golde heard that Sholem's father had forbidden their marriage, she burst into tears. Her mother hugged her, and said:

"There, there. The Briskers are just country nobodies. You can do better."

"But I don't want anyone else!" she sobbed. "I want to marry Sholem!"

That afternoon, Yakov Reiff went to see the District Magistrate.

"I want to rent Azriel Brisker's mill," he said.

"Oh," said the Magistrate. "Are the Briskers moving out?"

"They'll have to," said Yakov. "You're going to throw them out."

41

"But why should I do that?" said the Magistrate. "They're good honest people, and they've always paid their rent on time."

"Find an excuse," said Yakov. "Say they're stealing flour or something."

"But they're not," the Magistrate pointed out. "What if somebody asks me for proof?"

"Well," said Yakov, "Azriel has to sign a new contract every year, doesn't he?"

"Yes," said the Magistrate.

"So if you made next year's contract with me instead, the Briskers would have to leave at the end of this year."

"Yes," agreed the Magistrate, "I suppose they would. But I'd want a lot more rent." Of course, the real rents were set by the government: the Magistrate was planning to keep the extra money for himself.

"I'll pay whatever you ask!" promised the innkeeper.

So they drew up a contract; and the Magistrate wrote to the Briskers to tell them they had to move out by the end of the year. They were shocked: and they pleaded with him to change his mind.

"We've always been millers," they said. "We don't know how to do anything else. What will we live on if we don't have the mill?"

"That's not my concern," said the Magistrate with a shrug. "Maybe somebody in some other district has a mill to rent."

"But this is our home!" said Azriel's wife.

"It's not yours any more," said the Magistrate. "I've already signed a contract with Yakov Reiff. There's nothing to be done."

When they learned it was Yakov who was having them thrown out, they went straight round to the inn.

"Please, Yakov, forgive my refusal!" begged Azriel. "I'm sorry for the harsh things I said about you. Of course Sholem and Golde can get married."

"What?" sneered Yakov. "You don't have a mill any more. You're just a pack of beggars now. Why on earth would I let Golde marry a beggar?"

So the Briskers went sadly on their way, and the Reiffs moved into the mill. Poor Golde could not stop crying at the cruel way her parents had treated Sholem and his family; but Yakov and Feige ignored her, and told each other that she would soon get over it.

3:     *The demons*

What the Reiffs didn't know was that a family of river demons lived in the Horyń, just below Azriel's mill. The demons were cruel and spiteful beings who loved to torment humans, but they had never been able to hurt the Brisker family because of a blessing that had been placed on the mill years before. When the Reiffs moved in, the demons soon got to know of it in their deep dark pools, and they cackled and rubbed their clawed hands.

"Ha ha!" they crowed. "We can do as we like now!"

"Let's choke up the mill-wheel with weeds!" said one.

"Let's rip open the sacks and scatter flour over everything!" suggested another.

"Let's pinch and poke and shout in their ears, and never let them sleep!" giggled the littlest demon.

But that night when they went capering up to the mill, they found that the blessing was as strong as ever, and they couldn't cross the threshold. Groaning with disappointment, they dived back down to the bottom of the pool.

Meanwhile, Azriel Brisker had gone to consult a wise rabbi, who was known as the Holy Grandfather of Shipoli. He told the good old man all his troubles: and the rabbi answered:

"Do you remember, Azriel Brisker, many years ago, a wandering scribe came to your mill?"

"Yes," said Azriel. "There was a terrible storm that night and the poor man was lost. We gave him a hot meal and a bed for the night, and he blessed my house. After that we always had good luck, until now."

"I was that scribe," said the rabbi. "My blessing kept you safe from ghosts and demons, but it could do nothing about the wickedness of living men. I will write to Yakov Reiff, and tell him to give you back your mill: if he does not, I will take back my blessing."

So the Holy Grandfather wrote a letter, and Azriel Brisker carried it to the mill: but Yakov tore it up and threw it in his face.

"Why should I care for what some stranger says?" he scoffed. "What business is it of his anyway? We have our own rabbi in this village. Blessings and curses, indeed! What a lot of superstitious nonsense!"

So Azriel went sadly back to the rabbi; and the old man said:

"So be it. I lift my blessing from the mill: now any wizards and evil spirits can do what they like there."

And down in the gloom of their pool, the river demons heard his words; and they laughed and laughed and laughed.

There was a bath-house attached to the outside of the mill. There was a sunken stone tub there, fed by water from the river diverted through heated pipes; and the way in was down a wooden staircase from the family rooms above the mill.

The morning after the rabbi had lifted his blessing, Feige Reiff decided to go and bathe in this tub: but the demons had been there the night before, and taken half the slats out of the stairs. The moment she set foot on the staircase, it collapsed beneath her, and she went tumbling down into the Horyń River; and the demons seized her, crying:

"Haha! Haha! Now you will be our slave, and work for us down beneath the riverbed until the end of time!"

"My family will come and find me," said Feige.

"No they won't," promised the chief demon, "for they'll never know you're missing!"

And with that, she snapped her fingers, and changed herself into a perfect copy of Feige Reiff. And while the other demons dragged the real Feige down to their underwater lair, the chief demon mended the stairs, and went back up into the mill.

It was nearly time for lunch, and Feige had set out the food before she went down to the bath-house. When the demon saw such a fine meal laid out, she at once started guzzling it down. When Feige's children came in, they were shocked to see what they thought was their mother, slobbering and spitting food everywhere.

"Mother," said her little son, "why have you started without us?"

"Go away," said the demon, through a mouthful of potato. "This food is all for me."

"But we're hungry," said her younger daughter.

"Yaaagghhh!" howled the demon, and slapped them both so hard that they ran away crying. When Yakov came in, he said:

"What on earth has got into you, my dear? You've really upset the children."

But the demon gave a great roar, like a bull and a bear fighting; and Yakov ran off in a great terror. That night, the rest of the family slept downstairs in the mill, because they didn't dare go up to their rooms where demon-Feige was; and when they went for breakfast they found only a few scraps and crusts – the demon had eaten everything else.

They spent a miserable few days, living in the cold mill, spending all their money on food for the demon, and eating nothing but the scraps she left behind. But things were even worse for the real Feige, down below the bottom of the river. She had to spend every minute cleaning the demons' dank and dripping caves; but because they were under the river, there was always more muddy water pouring in, and they never got any cleaner. There was nothing to eat but water-weed, and only sharp rocks to sleep on: and she made up her mind to escape.

5:      *The doctor's visit*

At last, Golde said to her father:

"This has happened because you threw the Briskers out of their house! You must go to the Magistrate and ask him to put things back the way they were."

"Nonsense!" replied Yakov. "Your mother is ill. I shall fetch a doctor from Rivne. He will know what to do."

So the next day he set out for Rivne.

46

When Yakov had explained everything to the doctor, he hummed and hawed, and said:

"I'll have to examine your wife, but it sounds as if she won't want to let me. Can I hire some strong people in your village to hold her still in case she attacks me?"

"Oh yes," Yakov promised. So they hurried back to the village, and got four strong men together: then they went up to the mill.

The demon-Feige was busy making herself a big cauldron of soup when they arrived. The doctor peered round the door, and said softly:

"Mrs Reiff?"

At once, she picked up the pot and threw the hot soup straight in the doctor's face. He screamed in pain, and the four men rushed into the room to try to overpower her: but she bashed them over the head with her cauldron, and soon they all had to retreat.

"What do you think it is, doctor?" asked Yakov anxiously.

"I haven't the faintest idea," said the doctor. "But I'm not going in there again. You say she's been eating a lot; try keeping her food away from her." So the next day, Yakov didn't bring any food up: but demon-Feige smashed all the furniture and tore down the curtains, and ate those: so he gave in, and brought her her food as usual. He was beginning to wonder if Golde was right.

There was a shepherd in those parts who had a reputation as a magician: and the next day, Yakov went to fetch him.

"It sounds as if your wife's possessed by a demon," said the shepherd. "I'll see what I can do."

So Yakov brought him to the mill. The moment demon-Feige saw him, she knew he was a powerful wizard, and she hid her face with a scarf: but he walked right up and snatched it away, and looked her in the eyes. She hissed, and spat at him, and he backed away: and he said to Yakov:

"It's worse than I thought. That isn't one of the earth demons, who are easy enough to deal with. It's a water demon, and a very powerful one. There's nothing I can do."

"But don't you know anyone who can help me?" begged Yakov. "I must get my wife back! Did Azriel do this? Or his friend the rabbi?"

"They would have to be very great sorcerers," said the shepherd. "Tell me about them." So Yakov told the story: and when the shepherd heard that the rabbi had lifted his blessing from the mill, he said: "That must be it. The demons were obviously just waiting to get in. If you persuade the rabbi to bless your house again, the demon may leave: but I don't know how you'll get your real wife back."

6:     *Feige's escape*

Meanwhile, the real Feige had managed to sneak away from the demons' lair while they were out putting stones in horses' hooves and making milk go bad. But she didn't know her way through the caves, and she wandered for hours in the pitch black tunnels: and when she finally did find a way out, it led into the water. But there was no other way to escape: so she held her breath, and dived in.

The water was freezing and filthy, and flowed fast as the wind; and she was buffeted this way and that, bouncing off rocks, unable to breathe – but at last, she was washed up on the river bank in a forest.

There she was found by a party of fishermen.

"Which way to Radyvyliv?" she asked them. They frowned at her.

"Radyvyliv?" said one. "Where's that?"

"Don't be silly," she said. "It's the main town of this district."

"Radyvyliv..." said the oldest fisherman. "I do know a town of that name, out west somewhere. But it must be over four hundred kilometres away."

"What!" cried Feige. "Isn't this the Horyń River?" Though now that she thought about it, it looked much wider than the Horyń.

"This is the Dnieper," said the oldest fisherman. "You're in Kiev Province, only a few hours north of the great city."

Then Feige remembered that she had heard that time and distance worked differently in the world of demons: and she was horribly afraid that she might have been down there for hundreds of years. So she asked the fishermen what year it was: and they gave her a worried look, but they told her.

"Well," she thought to herself, "at least it's still the same year. But how will I ever get home?"

The fishermen couldn't help her; so she built a hut by the river, and started weaving baskets out of twigs. In the baskets, she put notes telling what had happened to her: then she dropped them into the river, and they were carried downstream to Kiev. Many different people found the baskets, and soon the story of the woman who'd been carried off by river demons spread throughout the city.

Before long, it reached the ears of a merchant who was about to set off for Poland. He was going to be passing through the Radyvyliv area: so he sent his servants into the forest to find Feige, and offered to take her with him.

When they came to the village, she ran at once to the mill. Her children cringed away in fear when they saw her, thinking it was the demon: but she swept them into her arms and kissed them, and they rejoiced, knowing that their mother had returned. Yakov wept for joy: and the whole family went together to seek out Azriel Brisker.

"Please get the rabbi to bless the mill again and make the demon leave," begged Yakov. "You can have the mill back; you can even have my inn if you want. Just get rid of the demon!"

"I don't want your inn," said Azriel. "Just my mill. And I want you to know, I was to blame as well as you. I shouldn't have been so proud, and believed all those rumours about you. I should never have forbidden our children's marriage."

So the Reiffs moved out of the mill, and went back to their inn in Radyvyliv; and the Holy Grandfather blessed the mill again. The moment that he spoke the words, the chief demon dived into the river and disappeared; and the Briskers moved back in.

Not very long after, Sholem and Golde were married: and the whole village rejoiced, and celebrated for days. They lived a long and happy life together: and their families never quarrelled again.

THE ADVENTURES OF TOM HICKATHRIFT

From an English chapbook

1:     *Tom's childhood*

Long ago, in the Isle of Ely, there lived a boy named Tom Hickathrift. His father was a serf who farmed the Abbot of Ely's land, and life was never easy: but when Tom was little, they had enough to live on.

But then England was invaded by the Normans, and William the Conqueror became King. When Ely fell, Tom's father was killed in the fighting, and the land he had farmed was taken away from the Abbot and given to a Norman knight.

When the knight found out that Tom's father was dead, he said:

"What good are a woman and a little boy to me? I need strong men to work my land." So he threw them out of their house.

They built a hut on the edge of the Fen and lived there, and Tom's mother took every job she could find to earn money and put food on the table. Tom grew and grew, until he was the biggest young man in Ely; and the bigger he grew, the more he ate, so that his mother had to work harder and harder to get food for him.

They slept on straw on the floor of the hut; it was nice enough when the straw was fresh and clean, but the longer it was down, the dirtier it got, and flies and fleas came in and made their homes there. One day, Tom woke up to find he'd been bitten all over: and he said:

"Mother, we need fresh straw."

"That's all very well," said his mother; "but I spent our last penny on beans to make pottage, and you ate it all up. How are we to buy straw without money?"

"We can ask Farmer Oswald if he's any to spare," said Tom.

"Well," said his mother, "I've no time to go over to Oswald's farm today. I have work to do. If you want fresh straw, you'll have to go yourself."

So Tom took a cart-rope and went off to Oswald's farm; and, finding the farmer in the threshing-barn, he said:

"I've come from my mother, to ask if you'll let us have a bundle of straw for the floor."

"Of course, Tom," said the farmer, who was a kind-hearted man. "Take as much as you can carry."

So Tom laid down his cart-rope on the floor, and started piling straw on top of it, armful after armful; and the farmer's foreman laughed at him, and said:

"Why are you building a haystack? You'll never carry that home."

But Tom ignored him, and kept on piling up the straw until there was a heap of it almost as big as him: then he tied the rope round the top of it and pulled it tight, to make a single bundle.

"Stupid boy," said the foreman. "It would take a cart and two horses to pull a bundle like that; no man could ever lift it."

But Tom lifted up the bundle, and put it on his back, and carried it home: and he mucked out the old straw and spread the lovely fresh straw over all the house. When it was done, there was some left over: so he took it into town and sold it. By the time his mother got home, the house was clean and sweet-smelling, and Tom had made almost as much money as she had.

2:     *Tom gets a job*

Soon all of Ely had heard that Tom had grown as strong as a giant; and everyone who wanted a heavy barrel carried up to the loft, or a cart held steady so that a broken-off wheel could be fixed, or a fallen tree hauled out of the road, came to him for the job.

One day Tom went to a fair, and there were all sorts of sports and games going on: wrestling, archery, axe-throwing, and a great deal more. Some of his friends said to him:

"You'd be good at this, Tom; have a go at throwing the hammer."

So Tom picked up the heaviest hammer, and threw it: and it went over the heads of the crowd, and over the fields, and landed in the River Ouse.

"That was my best hammer!" exclaimed Lokk the blacksmith, who had lent it to the fair. "You'll have to pay for that!"

"Don't worry," Tom's friends told him, "you can win the money at wrestling."

"But I don't know how to wrestle," said Tom.

Just then, a stout woman in rich clothes stepped out of the crowd, and said:

"I'll pay for the hammer."

"That's very kind of you," said Tom, "but who are you?"

"I'm Audrey the Alewife," she said. "I run a brewery in King's Lynn. I make more ale than I can sell in my town, so I want to start selling here in Ely and other towns, and maybe even over in Cambridge: but the roads are muddy and full of holes, and there are robbers and wild beasts about. I need a brave, strong man to take my dray over the Fens for me and deliver my ale: and I think you're the man I need. Do you want the job?"

"Yes please," said Tom.

So Tom Hickathrift went to work for Audrey the Alewife. He took the dray down to Swaffham and up to Hunstanton, and out to Spalding and over to Fakenham, and back to Ely where he'd come from: and nobody attacked him, because all the robbers and outlaws and trolls had heard of his great strength.

Audrey's ale was the tastiest in all the Fen country, and soon people were coming from even further afield to sample it. One day, when Audrey was out getting a new contract, a woman arrived who'd come all the way from Cambridge.

"My name is Thora," she said. "I'm the landlady of the White Dragon. We have brewers in Cambridge but none of them is very good. I've heard that you sell the best ale in the Fens: may I try some?"

"All right," said Tom: and he poured her a cup of ale, and took one for himself. As they drank, they talked and laughed, and Tom thought that he had never found anyone so friendly and easy to talk to before: and he was sad, because she lived on the other side of the Fens, and she was a landlady and he was only a drayman.

When Audrey came back, Thora said to her:

"It's true what I heard, this ale really is the best in East Anglia. Would you be able to send some as far as Cambridge?"

"I don't know about that," said Audrey. "Tom here is my only drayman, and Cambridge is a long way away. Why don't I sell you my recipe, and you can brew your own?"

"All right," said Thora: but Tom was sadder still when he heard that, because he wouldn't be able to take deliveries to the White Dragon and see her there.

3:      *The giant*

Once Thora had got the recipe and gone on her way, Audrey said to Tom:

"I've just had an order for a whole waggon-load of ale to go to the Red Horse in Wisbech: but you'll have to take the long road there."

"Why's that?" asked Tom. "Is the straight road across the Smeeth flooded?"

"No," said Audrey, "but it's too dangerous. There's a giant living on the Smeeth, and he robs every traveller who passes that way."

"Very well," said Tom, "I'll go the long way." But secretly, he decided to go the short way: for he thought it would be a very good thing if he could drive the giant away or kill him, so that travellers could go to and from Wisbech in peace.

So Tom set out for Wisbech with his dray. It took him most of the day to get there, because the Smeeth road was bad: and when he got close, the dray-horse smelt giant, and it whinnied in fear, and wouldn't go any further.

So Tom got down, and walked up the road. There were bones on the ground, of people the giant had killed; a smashed-up cart lay half sunk in the mud; and up ahead, near the giant's cave, was a great log gate across the road, blocking his way. For the first time in his life, Tom felt a little bit afraid: but he walked up to the gate, and set his shoulder to it, and pushed it open.

"Hoom!"

There came a dreadful roar: and out of the cave came the giant.

He was five metres tall, and had legs like tree trunks, and a great mass of shaggy hair like a lion's mane; he wore a shapeless tunic that looked as if it was made from the biggest turnip-sack in the world; he carried a club as big as a man, and he smelt like a stagnant pond.

"Who are you, little man?" he growled. "And what do you mean by opening my gate without permission?"

"I don't need permission," said Tom. "This is a public road."

"This is my road!" said the giant. "Nobody comes this way without paying me, and if they try, I bite their heads off!"

"You can try it," said Tom. "But I'm the famous Tom Hickathrift, the strongest man in East Anglia, and I'm not afraid of you."

"Graaagghhh!" screamed the giant: and he hefted up his club, and ran at Tom, swinging it wildly at his head.

Tom was standing next to the smashed-up cart: and he snatched up a wheel in one hand and half an axle in the other, and held them out in front of him to ward off the club. The giant swung at him, and hit the wheel, and made the rim of it crack: but Tom jumped forward and hit him with the axle, and he staggered back, moaning.

"Ha!" said Tom. "You haven't got at my ale yet, but it looks like you're already drunk!"

The giant came back, and tried again to hit Tom: but Tom dropped his wheel and skipped out of the way, so that the giant's club stuck in the mud. He leant down to try and pull it out: and Tom hit him so hard with the axle that he knocked his head clean off, and that was the end of the giant of the Smeeth.

Tom left the giant lying on the ground, and led his horse and dray through the gate and on into Wisbech; he found the Red Horse, and called out:

"I've brought the beer you ordered; and I've killed your giant."

"You've killed the giant?" cried the landlord; and people came out of the houses all around, saying:

"You've killed the giant? Show us, show us!"

So Tom took the townspeople out to the cave, and showed them the dead giant: and they danced and sang, and rejoiced that their oppressor was no more. Then they went into the cave, and found it full of gold and silver that the giant had stolen from unwary travellers: and they all said:

"The people who owned this are dead; Tom should have it all, and the cave and the land about it."

So Tom was made master of the giant's land: and, once he had taken the dray back to King's Lynn and told Audrey that he didn't need a job any more, he spent some of the treasure on building a neat little house in front of the cave, with a garden and a vegetable patch; and he sent for his mother to live with him there. But he gave the rest of the land to the people of Wisbech, to graze their animals on; and they sang songs about the brave and generous Tom Hickathrift. So his fame went through all of England, and even over the seas. And news even came to the land where the giants live: and when they heard that their friend had been killed in England, the giants were angry, and plotted revenge: but Tom knew nothing about that yet.

After this, instead of asking Tom for help with broken wheels and fallen trees, people came to him for really big problems. He was asked to drive out a pack of wolves who were stealing sheep on the Fens; to fight a monstrous bear; and one day a young girl came to him with a message from the people of Tilney St Lawrence.

"Our common land has been seized by a Norman baron, Lord Islington," said the girl. "We dare not fight his soldiers, but we will if you lead us."

So Tom went off to Tilney, and he tore down the enclosure fences, and he and the villagers drove the Norman soldiers out: and he said to Lord Islington:

"This common has always belonged to the people. If you try to steal from them again, you'll have me to deal with." And the wicked baron gnashed his teeth, but said nothing.

One morning, not long after this, Tom went out of his front door, and found a tinker and his dog in the garden.

"Excuse me," he said. "This is my garden."

"I hear you're the strongest man in East Anglia," said the tinker. "I've never lost a cudgel-fight, and I wondered if you were the man to beat me."

"I'll have a go," said Tom.

So they took up their sticks, and they bashed and battered and bopped and banged, until at last the tinker knocked Tom's stick out of his hand.

"You win," said Tom. "I've never lost a fight before. What's your name?"

"Harry Nonesuch," said the tinker.

"Well then, Harry Nonesuch," said Tom, "why don't you stay to tea?" And after that they became the best of friends.

Now that Tom was rich, he felt able to go courting Thora: and so he started visiting her in Cambridge once or twice a week, and very well they got on: and he hoped to ask her to marry him. But then, one day, he arrived at the White Dragon to find Lord Islington there.

"What are you doing here?" exclaimed the baron.

"What are *you* doing here?" said Tom.

"Don't speak to me like that, you jumped-up scoundrel!" snapped the baron. "Don't you know I'm a lord? I'm here to marry Thora."

"Does she want to marry you?" said Tom.

"What's that got to do with it?" said the baron. "My friend, the Earl of East Anglia, owns the land this inn is built on. If she doesn't marry me, he'll pull the White Dragon down, and she'll be ruined."

"You dirty dog!" shouted Tom.

"How dare you insult a lord?" said Lord Islington. "If you were a gentleman, I'd challenge you to a duel: but you're just a dumb English peasant, and you're not allowed to carry a sword."

"I'll fight you without one," said Tom; and the baron gave an evil grin.

"Very well," he said, thinking he would easily kill Tom if he had a weapon and Tom didn't.

So they went out into the courtyard of the inn: and the baron drew his sword, and lunged straight at Tom's chest. Tom jumped aside, and the baron rushed straight past him: and Tom wheeled round, and kicked Lord Islington in the seat of his trousers, so hard that he flew over the roof of the inn, and fell into a fishpond on the other side.

While Lord Islington was clambering out of the pond, cursing and pulling fish out of his clothes, Tom went back inside, and asked Thora to marry him: and she hugged him and kissed him, and said:

"Yes, of course I will!"

So it was a happy Tom who set off the next day for Wisbech, to make arrangements for the wedding: but as he was passing through the woods, two Norman soldiers jumped out and attacked him. He picked them both up, and knocked their heads together: then he carried them back to his house, and said:

"Who sent you to attack me?"

"Lord Islington," they told him. So he let them go; but he was worried, because he knew that the baron would never forgive him.

A date was set for Tom and Thora's wedding; and they invited Harry Nonesuch and Audrey the Alewife and Farmer Oswald and all their other friends. The only sad thing was that Tom's mother wouldn't be there, because she had died a little while before: but, in memory of her, Tom invited all the poor widows of Wisbech.

It was a wonderful day, with feasting and singing and dancing and drinking – Audrey supplied the ale for free –

and everybody was having a perfect time, until suddenly, a gang of ruffians with swords and axes appeared, and turned over a table full of cakes and pastries, and shouted out:

"Death to Tom Hickathrift!"

"I'm the man you're after," said Tom: but Harry Nonesuch said:

"You shouldn't have to fight on your wedding day."

Then, grabbing a sword from the nearest ruffian, Harry charged at the rest, swinging it round his head: and all the other guests followed him, roaring in anger. They soon put the villains to flight; and Thora said:

"We mustn't let this spoil our day. Carry on with the party!"

So they did, long into the night; but Tom knew that Lord Islington had sent the ruffians, and that sooner or later they would come back.

5:      *The rebellion*

After that, Tom and Thora lived in peace for a while; but soon all of England would be at war. For while King William was away in France, a group of Norman earls were plotting to seize control of the government: and they had secretly raised two armies, one in the west and the other in the east, right in the Fenlands where Tom and Thora lived.

One night, after they had gone to bed, they heard a frantic knocking at the door. They went down in their nightshirts to see who was there: and when they opened the door, who should be outside but the Sheriff of Cambridge.

"You have to help me," said the Sheriff. "The Earl of East Anglia's men have driven me out of my house. They're going through all the villages, making everyone bow down to the Earl's standard. Please, may I hide here?"

"Of course you may," said Thora. "But where's the Earl's army? In Cambridge?"

"No," said the Sheriff. "Most of it is based at Ely, under the command of Lord Islington." Then Tom was angry at the thought of the baron and his soldiers camping in the town where he grew up; and he said:

"Harry and I will deal with them." Then he called together the people of Wisbech and the Smeeth: and he said to them: "You all remember how Lord Islington tried to steal the common land at Tilney, and how his soldiers go about the country, bullying everybody and taking what they like. Well, now they want to make us all the Earl's slaves. I say we should go to Ely and throw them out!" And the people shouted their agreement.

So Harry and Tom led their band to Ely, picking up new followers in every village: and when they got there, Lord Islington came out to meet them, with a troop of soldiers behind him.

"What do you think you can do against us?" he sneered. "A gang of peasants with no armour? We'll chop you to mincemeat."

Then Tom, with a mighty roar, hurled himself at the evil baron: and he snatched him up by the ankles, and swung him round like a great club, and knocked down a whole row of soldiers; then he threw him out into the marshes, where his heavy armour pulled him down: and he sank to the bottom and was never seen again.

"The rest of you can go home," said Tom: and they slunk away, hanging their heads.

6:   *The Cyclops*

When King William got back from France, the Sheriff told him how Tom and Harry had defeated Lord Islington: and the King sent for them both, and Thora, to come to London. The Sheriff accompanied them to the Tower, where they were given splendid new clothes, and shown into the throne room: and King William said to them:

"Thanks to your courage, I am still King. I am going to make you both knights, and Mrs Hickathrift a lady, and award you a royal pension for the rest of your days." So he dubbed Tom and Harry knights, and gave them both fine swords and armour, and Thora a chain of gold: and they thanked him heartily.

King William threw a great feast in their honour, with roast boar and stuffed goose and pears stewed in wine: it was the finest food they had ever tasted. But while they were feasting, a messenger came hurrying in with urgent news.

You see, when news had reached the giant country of how Tom killed the Wisbech giant, the people had gone to their king to demand revenge. So the Giant King had sent his greatest warrior, Brontes the Cyclops, to attack England, and destroy the whole country to avenge the giant Tom had killed. Brontes had saddled up the enormous dragon that he always rode, put his iron mace on his shoulder, mounted the dragon, and spurred her into the air: and she had flown over the ice that guards the borders of Giantland, and over the angry sea, and down at last to England, where she landed in Kent. At once Brontes and the dragon had set about smashing and burning and destroying everything that they saw: and so the Sheriff of Kent had sent his fastest rider to London, to beg for help from the King.

The messenger burst in while the feast was in full swing, and blurted out the terrible news.

"Sir Thomas," said the King to Tom, "you are a famous giant-slayer. Will you deal with these monsters?"

"That I will," said Tom.

And so, at dawn the next day, he put on his new armour, took up his fine sword, and rode down to Kent. It wasn't hard to find Brontes' trail: the ground wherever he had been was burnt black by the dragon's fire. Soon Tom came up to the Sheriff's castle, and met the cyclops outside. Brontes was even bigger than the Wisbech giant, and he had hair like a nest of snakes, a beard like a tangle of rusty wire, and one great eye like a basin in the middle of his forehead.

"Hullo up there," called Tom. "I'm looking for the Sheriff of Kent."

"Well, you can't see him," snarled the cyclops. "He's stuck in this castle, and if he comes out I'm going to eat him alive."

"And who might you be?" asked Tom.

"I'm Brontes the Cyclops, the greatest warrior of Giantland!" shouted the monster.

"If you're such a great warrior," said Tom, "why are you waiting around for the Sheriff to come out? I'd have thought somebody as big as you would be able to push that flimsy little castle over."

"Hmm," said the cyclops. "You're right. I'll push it down, and squash him inside!" So he put his shoulder to the castle wall, and shoved.

What the cyclops hadn't noticed, and Tom had, was that the ground outside the castle was very muddy and slippery. Soon Brontes' feet began to slide, and he couldn't get a grip. He pushed harder, but he just slipped further: and while he was puffing away and going red in the face,

Tom rode up behind him, and stuck the end of his sword in the giant's bottom.

Brontes gave a yell of pain, and completely lost his footing. He fell flat in the mud: and before he could get up again, Tom rode up and cut off his head.

He soon chased the dragon away; and when the news got back to the land of the giants that Brontes had been killed, the giants decided that England was too dangerous to attack, and vowed not to go back there. Meanwhile, Tom rode back to London, and gave the cyclops' head to the King: and William said to him:

"Thomas Hickathrift, you are the bravest man in England. You and Lady Thora shall be the new Earl and Countess of East Anglia: and may you live in peace and contentment for the rest of your days."

So Tom and Thora went home in state, with a train of soldiers and servants and many treasures that the King had given them; and there were no wiser or kinder nobles in all of England, nor any better loved by their people. And just as the King had promised, they lived happily ever after.

THE FIVE SISTERS

From a Somali-Ethiopian folk tale

1:      *The wicked stepmother*

A little while ago, near the town of Jijiga in Ethiopia, there lived a poor man who had five daughters. He had a little patch of farmland, but needed to go hunting as well, because the farm wasn't big enough to keep them all. His wife had died some time before, and he wanted to marry again: so he proposed to a widow he knew.

"I'm sorry," she said. "I would love to marry you, but how would we ever survive? You have five hungry daughters to feed, and as they grow up they'll eat more and more. I can't be in a family that can't support itself."

So he went home, very sad; but he grew lonelier as the days went by, and at last he went back to the widow, and said:

"My oldest daughter Halima is old enough to get married. If she leaves, there'll only be four girls to support."

But she said:

"What! Send away the hardest worker and keep the four useless mouths? That's worse than supporting all five of them!"

"But what can I do?" said the poor man. "My other daughters are too young to get married, or to go out to work. I've always managed to keep them well enough – we are poor, but we aren't starving."

"But I don't want to be poor," said the widow. "I want fine clothes, and beef to eat. I won't marry you unless you send your daughters away – *all* of them."

"But where can I send them?" wondered the father.

She shrugged.

"That's your problem."

So he agreed to find some other place for his daughters: and he and the widow were married. He sent messages to all his relatives, to see if they could take the girls in, but none of them could. He went round all of Jijiga to see if anyone would offer them a home, but he found nobody.

Meanwhile, it had been a very dry year, and he'd had a poor harvest: and there really wasn't enough food for the seven of them. Every day, the larder got emptier: and every day, his wife got angrier that the girls were still there.

"I've tried everything," he said at last. "I can't find another home for them."

"Then they must find one for themselves," said his wife, "for they can't stay here."

"But I can't just throw them out!" said their father.

"No," agreed his wife. "They'd only come home. So take them out into the bush, and leave them somewhere so far away that they can't find their way back."

"But they'll die out there in the bush!" exclaimed their father. "There are lions and ogres and demons, and the sun is so hot they won't bear it!"

"They'll die here if the food runs out," their stepmother pointed out.

And at last, the wretched father agreed to abandon his daughters.

2:    *Lost in the bush*

He gathered them all together, and said:

"Girls, today I'd like you to come with me on the hunt. If I go beyond your sight, call to me, and I'll grunt like a camel so that you know where I am."

So they got their water bottles, and some bread and biltong to eat, and went with him out into the bush. He led them away from the tracks, across rocky ground; the sun beat down on their heads, and soon they were gasping at the heat. Their throats were dry and their feet were sore, and they just wanted to sit down; little Ikran, the youngest, was almost ready to cry.

At last they came to a great spreading tree, and their father said:

"Sit here in the shade, and wait for me."

So they sat down, very glad to be out of the sun and not have to walk any further; and their father unslung his rifle, and went off to look for game. There were jagged rocks and thorn bushes and little scrubby trees all around, and before long they had lost sight of him.

"Where has Father gone?" said Ikran. "Call him back!"

"He's just trying to catch a wild goat to eat," Halima told her. "He'll be back soon."

"No, call for him!" insisted Ikran. "I want to see him!"

So they called out "Father!"; and from behind a rock a little way away, they heard a grunt like a camel's. Ikran ran towards the rock, and there behind it she found her father.

"What do you want?" he said crossly. "You've scared the goats away."

"I just wanted to make sure you were still here," she said meekly.

"Well, I am," he said. "Go back to your sisters."

So Ikran went back to her four sisters under the tree; and they had their lunch, and passed the time telling stories. Every now and then they would hear the bang of their father's rifle, but it seemed further away every time. Only when they noticed that the sun was beginning to set did Halima say:

"Now we really ought to call Father back. He may have gone some way, so we should all shout together."

So they all shouted for their father: and they heard a grunt from behind a little tree, not too far away at all. They hurried over to the tree: but when they got there, they found a camel eating the leaves. They shouted again: but nobody replied. They climbed up on the tallest rocks, and little Ikran into the branches of the big tree, and they looked in all directions: but they couldn't see him anywhere. He had gone home, and left them out in the bush.

3:    *The ogre's daughter*

"How are we to get home?" moaned Maryam, the middle sister. "We are miles from the road, and none of us knows the way!"

"No," said Halima. "But whoever owns the camel might know. Look – it's tethered to the tree. Somebody left it there, and they're bound to come back for it."

So they waited next to the camel: and soon enough, they heard the baa-ing of a small flock of sheep. They looked up, and saw the sheep being driven along by a girl about Halima's age: she was very tall and broad-shouldered, and had pointed ears and yellow eyes.

"I'm frightened," said Ikran. "She looks like an ogre."

But Halima stood up and said:

"We're lost; our father has abandoned us in the bush. Soon the sun will set, and it will be very cold, and wild beasts and demons will come out: we need somewhere safe to stay the night.

"I am sorry," said the shepherd girl, whose name was Dalyad. "My house wouldn't be safe for you: my mother is an ogre, and she would eat you if she found you."

"How are you not an ogre, if your mother is?" asked Maryam.

"My mother didn't always hate humans," said Dalyad. "My father was human: but the people of his village drove him out for marrying an ogre, and he died. My mother swore to have revenge, and ever since then she has killed every

70

human she can catch. She is weak and sick now, but she is still very dangerous."

"But if we stay out in the open, we'll die anyway," said Halima. "Please hide us somewhere; it'll just be for one night."

"All right," said Dalyad. "I'll get the camel and the sheep to kick up a cloud of dust when we get near my mother's house, so that she doesn't see you: then you can hide in the sheepfold. Snuggle up to the sheep: their wool is thick and warm, and the walls of the enclosure are tall and strong to keep out lions and jackals. But you must leave first thing in the morning."

So the five sisters agreed; and they followed Dalyad and her sheep back to the ogre's house. The animals kicked up a cloud of dust, just as Dalyad had said, so that her mother didn't see the girls come in; and they hid in the enclosure with the sheep. Dalyad closed the gate, and went into the house.

A fearful ogre her mother was! Dalyad was tall, but her mother stood over two metres high; Dalyad's ears were pointed, but her mother's were long and hairy like a jackal's, and stood up above her head; Dalyad's eyes were yellow, but her mother's were fiery red. When she was well, she used to roam the bush, catching unwary hunters and eating them whole: but now she was frail and ill, and stayed in bed.

Her nose twitched when her daughter walked in.

"I smell people," she said.

"It's only me you can smell," said Dalyad.

"I'm hungry," said the ogre. "Go and find me a baby to eat."

"No," said Dalyad. "I've told you before, Mother, eating people is wrong. You can have a goat."

So she cooked a goat, and they ate it together; but afterwards the old ogre felt sick. She bandaged up her ears, which were aching badly, and went to sleep; while outside the five sisters snuggled down among the sheep.

4:    *In Dalyad's house*

That night, the old ogre finally died of her illness. When Dalyad found that her mother was dead, of course she was sad, but she couldn't help being relieved that she wouldn't eat any more people: and she went to the five sisters and said:

"Why don't you stay here and live with me? The house is big enough for all of us, and it's safe here now."

So they buried the ogre and all moved into her house, and they helped Dalyad to tend her sheep and grow her vegetables. When word got out that the ogre was dead, people started to visit them, and it wasn't long before Dalyad had a boyfriend, whose name was Mukhtar. He and his friends came visiting often, and one day one of them said to Halima:

"Before very long, Mukhtar and Dalyad will be wanting to get married. Why don't you marry me too, and we can all move to the city?"

"No thank you," said Halima. "I couldn't leave my sisters on their own." But after that she worried about what would happen if Dalyad did decide to leave.

Not long after that, Mukhtar did ask Dalyad to marry him and move to Addis Ababa.

"Of course!" she said. "We'll give this house to Halima and her sisters."

"Oh, how happy we will be!" exclaimed Mukhtar. "I can't wait until we have children – I want at least seven!"

"Oh, no," said Dalyad. "I can't have more than five, for my mother told me that if I should have six I would turn into a true ogre like her."

"All right," said Mukhtar, "five."

So they gave the sisters the house, and moved to the city: and they did have five beautiful children, and lived very happily.

Meanwhile, Halima called her sisters together, and said:

"I think we should move back to Jijiga. If we sell this house and all the sheep, we can afford to buy a house in town and set up a bakery. Baking is an easier life than sheep farming."

They all agreed: so they put the house and farm up for sale. It didn't take them long to find a buyer: and they made plenty of money, enough to set up their bakery and have a bit left over. They lived in an apartment above the bakery; the eldest four all worked together making bread, and Ikran went round with a barrow and delivered it to their customers; and the business did very well.

5:     *The python*

One day, after doing her rounds delivering bread, Ikran was feeling very thirsty: so she went to the well to get some water. What she didn't know was that a monstrous rock python lived in that well: it had caught and eaten many unwary people and animals. It lay in wait near the bottom, and when it saw the water bucket begin to move upwards, it knew that there was somebody at the top: so when Ikran hauled up the bucket, the python came rushing up after it, grabbed her, and pulled her down to its cave at the bottom of the well.

Luckily for Ikran, the beast wasn't hungry right then: it had caught her to save for later. So it trapped her in its lair, but didn't eat her yet. The great snake's den was a sight to see: bones lay all around, but there was also a great pile of treasure that it had taken from its victims. Ikran sat shivering on the heap of gold and jewels, wondering how she was going to escape.

When she didn't come home, her sisters were terribly worried: and Halima went out into town, and asked all their customers if they had seen her little sister. They all said she had been round, delivered their bread, and gone on her way. At last, she came to the well, and saw Ikran's barrow by the side of it: and she cried out:

"Oh, how terrible! She must have been eaten by the rock python!"

Down in the cave at the bottom of the well, Ikran heard her sister's voice. The python had fallen asleep: so she wriggled out of the hole, and started trying to climb up the inside of the well, shouting:

"I'm still alive! Save me!"

She soon found that she kept losing hold of the stones, and slipping back down into the water: because the cunning python had smeared the walls of the well with soap to stop her escaping. When the snake heard her shouting, it woke up, and slithered after her: but Halima had heard her, and shouted down the well:

"Catch hold of the bucket, and I'll pull you up!"

So Ikran grabbed the edge of the bucket, and Halima cranked the handle as fast as she could: and because the snake was slowed down by the soapy walls, she managed to pull her sister safely out of the well, just ahead of its snapping jaws. They hurried home, and told their story: and all the girls hugged Ikran.

"That python has to be dealt with," said Halima.

So the next day, they all went to the well at a time when they knew the python would be awake and looking out for prey: and Ikran pulled the bucket up. The snake, who was watching and waiting for the bucket to move, came shooting after it once again: but Halima was waiting behind Ikran with a machete, and the moment the snake reached the top of the well, she rushed forward and cut off its head. Then Ikran stood on the bucket, and her sisters lowered her down into the well: and she went into the snake's lair, brought out all the gold and jewels she could carry, and filled the bucket with them. Then her sisters pulled her back up.

Thanks to the python's treasure, the five sisters were now the richest women in Jijiga. They bought a bigger house, and moved out of their apartment above the bakery: and a fine life they had.

Meanwhile, their father and stepmother were in a very bad way. After he had abandoned the girls, his crops had all failed, and he had had to sell the farmland: and soon the money was all gone, and they lost their home, and became beggars wandering the streets of Jijiga. One day, they happened to knock on their daughters' door to ask for food.

It was Ikran who opened the door; and when the two beggars recognised her, they fell down on their knees and begged her to forgive them.

"Of course I forgive you," she said. "But I can't speak for my sisters; you'll have to ask them too. Come in, and I'll fetch them."

So she got the other four together, and they saw the pitiful state their parents had been reduced to: and they agreed to forgive them for all the wrong they had done. They gave them a bath and some fine new clothes, and allowed them to live in their old apartment and work in the bakery; and they all lived happily ever after.

GUIMARA, THE GIANT PRINCESS

From a Brazilian folk tale

1:     *The wandering knight*

High in the Sierras of southern Brazil, there was once a land ruled by giants.

The native people knew to keep well away from the giants' country: for the giants were quarrelsome bullies, and used to kidnap passing humans to be their servants. But when the Portuguese came to those parts, they sent many expeditions into the high country, with muskets and pikes and cannons, to try to conquer them. At last the King of the Giants ordered a wall to be built all around his country, to keep the invaders out: and into the work of building that wall, he put nearly all of his magical power, for he was a great sorcerer. He built it around the Giants' City, and the lake where the Isle of Wild Beasts stood, and the richest soil of the Sierras, which the giants farmed: and he closed the gates and shut out the human world. When the wall was completed, it was as high and strong as a range of mountains, and nobody could see the top of it, for it stretched up into the clouds.

So the giants lived in their hidden country, behind the great wall, and never saw humans, native or Portuguese; and they never saw any other giants, either, for none came visiting any more. Their life became boring; there were not many of them left, and most of them were getting old; and they had forgotten most of their magic.

There were hardly any young giants left: but the King did have a daughter, Princess Guimara. She had been born after the wall was built, and had never seen the world outside. Her parents loved her, and spoiled her, and taught her magic: she became an even greater enchanter than her father, though he would never admit it. But she was still sad at being trapped behind the great wall, and loved to listen to older giants' stories of the great rainforests to the north, with their beautiful flowers and their deadly snakes, and of the strange men in iron coats who had come out of the east. She especially liked any story about humans: she wasn't sure if they really existed, but she hoped they did, and wished she had been born human instead of a giant: their lives sounded so much fun to her.

One day, a party of Portuguese noblemen from São Vicente went hunting in the Atlantic Forest; and one of them, a young knight named Dom João, became lost. He wandered far trying to find his friends, and found that he had come out the northwestern side of the forest, and up into the Sierras.

He knew he should turn back: but ahead of him he could see a strange sight. From out of the scrub, there reared up a huge cliff face, smooth and dark like smoked glass, and he couldn't see the top of it. It was the giants' wall. Dom João had never seen anything like it, and he felt he had to investigate.

So he rode up to the foot of the wall: and a great voice boomed out from above him, saying:

"Who are you, little man, and what are you doing here?"

"I am a knight," replied Dom João, "and my name is João."

"A knight you may be," replied the voice, "but you're my prisoner now. I can't let you go back to the coast and tell your people where the land of the giants is hidden." For the voice belonged to the King of the Giants.

He had been looking down from a high window, and had seen the knight ride up out of the forest: and now he unbarred the great gate, for the first time in years, pushed it open, and came out.

Dom João had never seen such a creature as the Giant King; he seemed almost as big as the wall itself. He reached down, and picked up the knight in one hand, and his horse in the other; and he carried them back into the land of the giants, and shut the gate behind him. Dom João was trapped.

2:    *Dom João meets Guimara*

The Giant King walked back up to his palace, and called out to the Queen and Guimara, saying:

"Wife! Daughter! I've caught a human; come and have a look at him!"

The Queen wasn't terribly interested, and didn't hurry: but Guimara rushed out of the palace as fast as she could.

"Where is he?" she asked breathlessly. "Show me!"

The Giant King held up the Portuguese knight: and Guimara gasped.

"He's beautiful," she said. "Just like a real person!"

"I *am* a real person!" snapped Dom João.

"He can talk!" exclaimed Guimara. "I never knew they could talk; I thought that was just a story. Are they all as big as this? I thought they were tiny, like little hairless monkeys, but he'd almost come up to my knee."

"This is a very ordinary human," said the Giant King.

"Well, he's extraordinary to me," said Guimara, "because he's the only one I've ever seen. Can I keep him?"

"He's going to be our servant," replied her father. "In the old days, we used to catch lots of humans, and make them do all the work around Giant City."

"I wish I'd lived back then," sighed Guimara. "It would have been fun to have so many humans around. Come on, little man, I'll show you round the palace." And she lifted Dom João out of her father's hand, and set him down on the ground.

Guimara chatted away as she showed the knight around; and she asked him all the questions she could think of about humans and the world outside. He answered as best he could: and she thought that she had never met anyone she liked so much.

Dom João thought the same thing about her, and he wished they were the same size, so that he could court her: but he didn't say anything. After he'd been shown round, the Giant King put him to work, cleaning the stables, mending pots and pans, and doing all the work the giants didn't like to do: and he stayed there a long time. In all that time, the only giant who was ever good to him, or even spoke to him except to give him orders, was the Princess Guimara: and they grew more and more fond of each other every day.

3:     *Impossible tasks*

One day, the Giant Queen went to her husband, and said:

"How do you not see what's happening? Our daughter has fallen in love with the human slave."

"Don't be ridiculous," said the Giant King. "He's so *tiny.*"

"Nevertheless," said the Queen, "they are in love. Do you want her to marry a human?"

"Of course not," said the King.

"Then you must find an excuse to get rid of him," said the Queen.

So the King of the Giants thought deeply; and he came up with a plan. He sent for Dom João, and said to him:

"You've been very good at your work so far."

"Thank you," said the knight.

"But I've heard you've been boasting you could do even more," said the King.

"Well," said Dom João, "cleaning the floors doesn't take much skill; I'm sure I could do something more difficult."

"What about building?" said the Giant King, with a cruel smile spreading across his face.

"I've helped to put up some sheds before," said Dom João. "I could do that."

"I want you to tear down my palace and rebuild it facing the other way," said the Giant King. "And I want you to do it by dawn tomorrow."

Dom João realised that the King had tricked him. There was no way he could turn the whole palace around, even in a year, never mind a single night. He trudged sadly out of the Giant King's hall, head hanging low.

Guimara was waiting outside.

"What's the matter?" she asked. "What did my father say?"

"He wants me to tear down the palace and rebuild it facing the other way, by dawn tomorrow," said Dom João. "How can I do that? It's impossible. Only an enchanter could do it."

"Exactly," said Guimara: "and I *am* an enchanter. Leave it to me, and I'll make it happen: but my parents must never know I helped you."

So, that night, the Giant King moved everybody out of the palace, and told Dom João to get on with tearing it down.

"Oh, I don't need to start yet," he said. "I'll wait until nearer dawn."

He and Guimara waited until the King and Queen and all the giants had gone to sleep: then she sang a spell, and the palace took itself apart brick by brick, turned around, and rebuilt itself, facing the other way. So when the giants awoke, they found that it had been turned round, just as the Giant King had asked.

The Giant King was startled to see the palace turned round, and he strongly suspected that the Princess had had a hand in it: but he couldn't prove it, and he had to admit that the job he'd given Dom João had been done.

"Well," he said grudgingly, "it'll do, I suppose. But now the palace faces the Isle of Wild Beasts. I don't want to look at that all the time. Clear all the beasts off it, and turn it into a garden; and do it by dawn tomorrow, or I'll squash you."

"That should be easy enough," said Dom João. "But I'll do it tonight; I need to rest now, because turning the palace round all on my own has tired me out."

So he went and had a sleep; then he told the Princess of the new task her father had given him.

"That shouldn't be too hard," she said.

So, that night, when all the other giants were asleep, Guimara cast a spell: and she set to work the jaguars and the howler monkeys, the caimans and the anacondas, the titis and the tapirs, and all the beasts that lived there, to clear away the trees and scrub, and plant bright flowers, and build a great silver fountain in the centre of the island: then she released all the animals through the great gate of her father's land, to return to the forests where they truly belonged. So it was that, when her parents awoke, they found the palace facing a gorgeous garden, the likes of which they had never seen before.

"This is our daughter's doing," said the Queen. "Setting the human impossible tasks is never going to work: Guimara is obviously a great enchantress, and whatever you think of, she'll be able to do."

The Giant King growled, and said:

"Don't worry about the human: I'll find a way to deal with him."

4:     *Escape*

All that day, the Giant King paced back and forth with a terrible frown on his face: and Guimara was frightened, for she had never seen her father so angry. She

83

was afraid he might kill Dom João: so she went to the knight, and said to him:

"We must run away tonight, it's not safe for you to stay here any longer. My father's horse is the swiftest in Giantland: meet me in the stables at midnight, and we'll steal it, and escape back to the coast and your people."

So that night they crept down to the stables, taking Dom João's musket from where the King had put it away when he captured him, and let the King's horse out of his stall. The horse might not have gone with strangers, but he had known Guimara since she was small (for a giant), and Dom João had been cleaning out his stable every day for months: so he let them saddle him, and get on his back, and they rode out through the gate of the giants' city, and away across the Sierras.

When the sun rose the next day, the Giant King's servants found that the Princess was not in her bed: and they ran to tell their master and mistress. The King and Queen soon worked out that Guimara had fled with Dom João: and the Queen said:

"Take my horse; it's nearly as fast as yours, and doesn't tire so easily. They'll have ridden down towards the Atlantic Forest, for Dom João comes from the Portuguese settlements on the far side."

So off rode the Giant King on the Queen's horse, as fast as they could go. The Queen was right: the stolen horse had grown tired, and Guimara and Dom João had stopped for breakfast at the edge of the Atlantic Forest. When the King came thundering down from the Sierras, however, Guimara heard him coming, and exclaimed:

"That's my father!"

"What will we do?" wondered Dom João. "There's nowhere to hide!"

"Oh yes there is," said Guimara. "Horse, be a brazilwood tree! Saddle and bridle, be a bed of onions! Musket, be a Blue Silk butterfly! João, be an old gardener! And I will be a pond."

Immediately as she spoke, everything she named changed its shape: so that when the King of the Giants rode up to the edge of the forest, all he saw was an old gardener, tending his onions next to his beautiful silvery pond, while a butterfly flapped lazily around a brazilwood tree.

"Tell me, old man," said the Giant King, "have you seen a young giantess ride this way with a little human man?"

"Oh, no, I've seen nothing at all," said Dom João. "Don't you like the fine smell of my onions, though?"

But the Giant King, who hated onions, held his nose; and he thought to himself:

"If they'd come this way, this gardener would surely have seen them. They must have taken another road." So he rode off back to the giants' city, while Guimara changed herself and Dom João, the musket, the horse, and the saddle and bridle, back into their own shapes, and they rode on through the Atlantic Forest.

But when the Giant King came home, and told his wife what had happened, she exclaimed:

"What a fool you are! Don't you see that that gardener must have been Dom João in disguise? Guimara is an enchantress, remember: she can change the shapes of things. I dare say she was the butterfly or the tree. Ride after them, and don't let them get away again!"

So the King set out, and rode as fast as he could. He came down from the Sierras to the edge of the forest, but the gardener and his onions and his pond and the butterfly and the brazilwood tree had all gone: and he knew then that his wife must have been right. He plunged into the forest, and crashed through the trees, towards the other side.

When Dom João and Guimara had left the Atlantic Forest behind them, they had stopped again, to have lunch. But when Guimara heard the crashing of her father forcing his way through the trees, she knew that she needed to use her magic powers again: so she said:

"Horse, be a bell; musket, be a prayer book; saddle and bridle, be an altar; João, be a priest; and I will be a church."

So it was that, when the Giant King came out of the forest, he found a church there, and a priest with bell and prayer book in his hands, praying at the altar.

"Tell me, Father Priest," said the Giant King, "have you seen a giantess ride this way with a young human knight? He may have been disguised as a gardener."

"I have seen nothing, my son," said Dom João. "Peace be with you."

So the King of the Giants turned round again, and rode home, thinking that he would never catch the couple now. Meanwhile, Guimara turned herself and Dom João and the musket and horse and saddle and bridle back into their own shapes: and she said to the knight:

"I believe we can make it to your city before my father comes after us again, and then we'll be safe. You will have to go into the city ahead of me, because your people are afraid of giants, and won't want to let me in: but whatever happens, keep your mind fixed on me, because the further we get from my father's kingdom, the weaker my giant-magic gets."

So they rode on towards Dom João's city; while the Giant King went home and told his wife what had happened.

"Of all the fools in the world, you are the worst!" yelled the Queen. "Don't you see that the priest was Dom

86

João again? Give me the horse: I'll go after them. If they haven't got to the city yet, I'll bring them back: but if they have, that's the end of that, because our magic has no power there, and even we can't fight an army of humans with armour and guns."

So she took her horse, and set off to catch her daughter and the human knight.

5:    *Guimara becomes human*

The Queen of the Giants rode like the wind: over the Sierras, and down into the Atlantic Forest; along the path where her husband had broken so many branches, and down into the plains beyond, towards the coastal cities where Dom João's people lived. It was nearly dusk, and the knight and the Princess had a good head-start: but she could see them in the distance ahead of her, just coming up to the gates of the knight's own city of São Vicente.

But Guimara heard her mother coming: and she took a handful of dust, and threw it in the air, saying:

"Dust, be the blackest storm cloud there ever was!"

And the dust turned into a storm cloud, and it thundered and roared, and hurled lightning and rain at the Queen of the Giants, until she was soaked and dazzled and didn't know where she was. There was no way she could ride through that storm: so while she was blundering around, trying to find somewhere to shelter, her daughter and Dom João came to the gates of the city.

As they had agreed, Dom João went in first, while the Princess and the horse waited at the gates. He had been terribly homesick, and he was delighted to see his own city again: and when his friends saw him, and shouted:

"João! You're alive!", he was so happy, and so busy hugging them, that for a moment he forgot all about Guimara.

"Where have you been?" asked his friends. "How did you get back here?"

So he told them all about the land of the giants, and how he had brought back a giant princess, and she was waiting at the gates: and they were all very excited, and begged to be allowed to meet her. So he took them all to the gate of the city, where he had left Guimara.

The Princess was still waiting there: but she wasn't a giant any more! She had shrunk right down to an ordinary human size. When Dom João saw this, he was amazed: and he said:

"How did this happen?"

"You must have stopped thinking about me while you were in the city," she said. "It's just as well you remembered me when you did, or I'd have vanished away altogether! But now I shall always be a human size – just as I always wanted to be!"

So she went into the city with Dom João; while her mother plodded back to Giantland, soaking wet, and said to the King:

"Our daughter is cleverer than either of us, and brave and loyal too. We were wrong to fight her: if she wants to marry a human, we should let her."

The people gave a big party to welcome the couple: and not long after that, they were married, and they lived happily ever after.

www.ingramcontent.com/pod-product-compliance
Lightning Source LLC
Chambersburg PA
CBHW070532130626
46555CB00003B/1377